This Topsy and Tim book belongs to

_____

This title was previously published as part of the *Topsy and Tim Learnabout* series
Published by Ladybird Books Ltd
80 Strand London WC2R ORL
A Penguin Company

3 5 7 9 10 8 6 4 2

ISBN-13: 978-1-84646-476-8
ISBN-10: 1-84646-476-5

Printed in China

Topsy + Tim

Storytime
Collection

Jean and **Gareth Adamson**

Contents

Topsy+Tim

At the Farm

Topsy and Tim and Mummy were on
their way to Rosemary Farm. They
were going to see Mummy's friend
Mrs Stewart, the farmer's wife.

14

"May we help on the farm?"
asked Topsy.
Mrs Stewart gave them two
egg-boxes.
"Go along to the hen-house,"
she said, "and choose twelve
nice eggs from the hens' nests
to take home."

Some hens came to greet
Topsy and Tim and a duck
quacked cheerfully.
Topsy found some ducklings
learning to swim in an old bath.

A loud hissing noise startled Topsy
and Tim. Four big, angry-looking
geese were moving towards them.
"We'd better run into the hen-house,"
said Tim.

The hen-house felt safe, but it was very gloomy. Soon their eyes grew used to the dark and they could see plenty of eggs in the hens' nests. Topsy chose six big eggs to fill her box. Four were white and two were brown.

The angry geese were on the path back to the farmhouse, so Topsy and Tim could not go that way.

They climbed the wall instead, being very careful with their eggs.
"Let's go back to the farmhouse this way," said Tim.

24

Topsy and Tim were
in the cows' meadow.
They did not know which way to turn.
Then they saw Farmer Stewart.
"I'm about to take these cows to the
milking-sheds," said Farmer Stewart.
"Will you give me a hand?"

Topsy and Tim helped Farmer Stewart
take the cows to the milking-sheds,
although the cows knew the way
themselves.
"Can we help milk the cows?"
asked Topsy and Tim.

"We will soon do that with our machines, thank you," said Farmer Stewart. "I've got a special job for you, though, if you'd care to help."

Farmer Stewart took a bucket of new milk. He led Topsy and Tim to a smaller shed.

There was a baby calf in the shed. "Poor thing. It wants this milk," said Farmer Stewart, "but it can't drink. It only knows how to suck. Put your eggs down somewhere and then you can teach the calf how to drink from the bucket."

Farmer Stewart showed Topsy what
to do. She dipped her finger in the milk.
Then she let the calf suck her milky
finger.
The calf sucked so hard that Topsy
felt nervous.

"Don't worry, it won't bite," said Farmer Stewart. Next, Topsy put her hand into the bucket. The calf went on sucking Topsy's finger until her hand and its nose were both in the warm milk. Then it was Tim's turn to feed the calf.

The calf soon discovered
how to drink from the
bucket without any help.
Topsy and Tim ran back
to the farmhouse to tell
Mummy all about it.

It was time for Topsy and Tim to go home. As they walked down the lane they heard a tractor behind them. It was Farmer Stewart.

"Here are the eggs you forgot,"
he said, "and here is a big carton of
cream for your tea, because you were
so good and helpful at the farm."

Topsy+Tim

Meet the Firefighters

One morning when Topsy and Tim
were on their way to school, they
heard a fire engine coming.

It raced past them, sirens sounding and blue lights flashing. All the other traffic got out of the way. Everyone knew that the firefighters were hurrying to put out a fire.

"Kerry's dad is a firefighter," said Topsy.
"I expect he is on that fire engine."

But Kerry's dad was not on the fire
engine. It was his morning off and
he was taking Kerry to school.
Topsy and Tim told him about the
fire engine they had seen.
"They're called fire appliances, not
fire engines," said Kerry.

"There's an open day at my fire station on Saturday," said Kerry's dad. "Would you like to come and see all our fire appliances?"
"Yes, please," said Topsy and Tim. On Saturday, Topsy and Tim and Mummy set out for Bellford Fire Station.

There were lots of children at the fire station. Firefighters in yellow helmets were looking after them.

Topsy and Tim soon found Kerry
and her dad.
Kerry was waiting to go up on a
long turntable ladder. Topsy and
Tim wanted to go up too.
A firefighter helped them all into a
cage on the end of the ladder. He
gave them safety helmets to wear.

A firefighter at the back
of the appliance pulled
a lever and the ladder
started to go up.

It grew longer and longer and went higher and higher, until the people on the ground looked as small as toys.
"We hose water down on to burning buildings from up here," said the firefighter.
"And you rescue people from high windows and roofs," said Kerry.

When they came down from the ladder,
Mummy bought them each a little
firefighter's helmet.
"I'm going to be a firefighter when
I grow up," said Kerry.
"Can girls be firefighters?" asked Topsy.
"I don't think so," said Tim.

"Yes, they can!" said the lady who was selling the toy helmets.

"I'm a firefighter, just like Kerry's dad. Women can be firefighters, but they have to be as strong and as brave as the men."

To show how strong she was, she gave Tim a fireman's lift.

Kerry's dad took them to see how
the fire station worked.

"When there is a fire and someone
phones 999," he said, "we get
the message on a fax machine. A
loudspeaker tells us where to go
and which appliances to take."

"Alarm bells ring and the firefighters
run to the appliances. If they are
upstairs they slide down a pole. It's
quicker than running down the stairs."

Kerry's dad lifted the children into
the cab of a big fire appliance.
They pretended to drive to a fire.

Near the big fire appliance was
a much smaller one.
"Is that a baby fire engine?"
asked Tim.
"It's a van full of rescue
equipment," said Kerry's dad.
"We take it to accidents and
rescue people from crashed
cars and trucks."

Kerry's dad showed them the tall tower where the firefighters practised with their ladders and hoses.

"When we have finished we hang the hoses in the tower to dry," he told them.

Next to the tower was a room that had been on fire. It made their noses tickle.

"We make smoky fires in there," said Kerry's dad. "Then we practise putting them out and rescuing people. We have to wear masks and carry tanks of air on our backs, or we would choke."

Kerry took Topsy and Tim into a
showroom full of fire dangers. It
looked like an ordinary living room.
"See if you can spot where fires
could start," said Kerry.
Tim spotted a cigarette on an
armchair seat.
"That could start a fire," he said.

Topsy spotted a box of matches on
the floor.
"A naughty little child might start a
fire with those," she said.
"And that electric heater should be
behind a fireguard," said Mummy.

Mummy spotted
more fire dangers
near a kitchen stove.
"Are smoke-detectors
any use?" she asked
Kerry's dad. "I think I
ought to get one."
Kerry's dad showed them a smoke-
detector and made it work. It made loud
BLEEP-BLEEP-BLEEP noises.

"If there was a fire in your home one night, the smoke-detector would wake you up," he said.

"We've got one," Kerry told Topsy.

It was time to go home, but before
they went, Kerry's dad gave them
one last treat.
It was a ride round the fire station
yard on a children's fire appliance.
The clever firefighters had made it
specially for their open day.

Topsy+Tim

Go to the Park

One sunny day, Topsy and Tim and
Mummy set off for the park with a
picnic for themselves and two big
bags of bread for the ducks.

The ducks were pleased to see
Topsy and Tim.

Feeding the ducks made Topsy and
Tim feel hungry.
"Let's go and find a place to have
our picnic," said Mummy.

They ate their picnic
sitting on a park
bench. Topsy had
peanut butter
sandwiches, crisps
and some orange
juice. Tim had
marmite sandwiches,
crisps and apple juice.

When they had finished, there was
a lot of rubbish left.
"What do we do with that?"
asked Mummy.
"Put it in the bin!" shouted Topsy
and Tim.
"Let's go to the swings now," said Tim.
"I'll race you there," said Topsy, and
off they ran.

When they reached the playground,
it was already full of children.
All the swings were taken.

"Hello, Topsy and Tim," called someone high in the air. It was their schoolfriend Kerry on one of the swings. "Hello, Kerry!" called Topsy, running towards her.

Kerry's mum grabbed Topsy and pulled
her back.
"You nearly got bumped
on the head," she said.
"You must never go
close to swings,"
said Mummy.

It wasn't long before
Topsy and Tim and
Kerry were having
lovely swings
together, all in
a row.

"Now let's have a go on the seesaw," said Tim, when they were tired of swinging. Topsy and Kerry sat at one end of the seesaw and Tim sat at the other, but Tim got stuck up in the air.

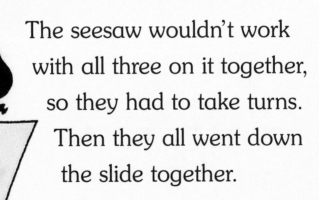

The seesaw wouldn't work
with all three on it together,
so they had to take turns.
Then they all went down
the slide together.

At last they
had had enough
fun in the playground.
They wandered back
to the grassy part of the park.
"I wish we'd brought a
ball to play with," said Tim.

"Surprise, surprise," said Kerry's
mum and she opened her bag and
tipped out a big, bouncy ball. Soon
Tim and Kerry and Topsy were hot
and happy, playing ball
on the grass.

Suddenly a big dog came running
across the grass. It caught the ball in
its mouth and leaped around with it.
"Drop it!" said Tim in a stern voice.
The dog dropped the ball and stood
wagging its tail.

"Good dog," said Tim and he put out
his hand to pat the dog.
"Don't touch the dog, Tim," said
Mummy. "You must never pat a
strange dog. It might bite you."

"I wish that dog would go away,"
grumbled Topsy. "It's spoiled our
game of football."
Just then the dog heard its owner
calling. It gave a cheerful bark and
ran off.

"It's time to go," said Mummy.
Topsy and Tim waved goodbye to
Kerry and her mum and they all
began to walk back to the park gates.

On the way, they had to pass the park cafe.

"I'm very hot," said Tim.

"I'm boiling," said Topsy.

"Would an ice cream cool you down?" asked Mummy.

"Ooh, yes," said Topsy and Tim.

Topsy and Tim and Mummy ate their ice creams as they walked through the park. When they went past the pond, a crowd of ducks waddled after them, hoping for a bit of cornet.

"Sorry, ducks, it's all gone," said Topsy.
"But we'll bring you lots more bread
next time we come," promised Tim.

Topsy+Tim

Look After Their Pets

Topsy and Tim's smallest pet was
Tubby mouse. Tubby was really Tim's
mouse but Topsy played with him too.

Every evening, after school, Tim put
a teaspoonful of crushed oats and
sunflower seeds into Tubby's dish.
Sometimes he gave Tubby treats,
like a piece of bread soaked in milk
or water, or bits of carrot or apple.
Tubby liked his treats.

Tubby liked to play outside his cage.
Twice a week, Mummy helped
Tim to clean out the cage, while
Topsy kept an eye on Tubby. Mummy
washed the cage clean. Tim spread
new sawdust on the floor and put
fresh hay in Tubby's sleeping box.

"I'll fill Tubby's water bottle,"
said Topsy one evening.
"No," said Tim. "He's my
mouse, so I fill his water bottle."
Topsy cupped her hands and
gently scooped Tubby up.
"I wish I had a mouse," she said.

"We don't want another mouse," said
Mummy. "They might have lots of
babies and we wouldn't be able to
look after them properly."
"I'd look after them," said Topsy.
"No," said Mummy and that was that.

Topsy went to feed the goldfish, Sam and Roundabout. Topsy liked them, but they weren't as much fun as a mouse.

Sam and Roundabout lived in a proper, rectangular fish tank. It stood in a shady corner of the room. Dad had fixed some water weed to small rocks with elastic bands. Sam and Roundabout liked to nibble the weed.

"Mummy," said Topsy, "the fish
need more water."
Mummy floated a piece of
clean paper on the water.

She gave Topsy a jug of fresh water to pour gently on to the paper. "That stops the tank getting stirred up," she said.

Topsy filled the tank very
carefully. Then she
took the paper
out. Sam and
Roundabout
swam happily in
their clean water.

Topsy gave them a little pinch of
fish food. She knew she mustn't
overfeed them.
"Don't forget to put the cover back
on the tank," said Mummy.
"We don't want Kitty to put her
paw in and catch them."

Topsy and Tim went
into the garden to
look after Wiggles,
their black and
white rabbit.

"I'll put Wiggles in his run. Then we can clean his cage," said Tim.

"You mustn't pick him up by his ears," said Topsy.

"I know that!" said Tim. Tim lifted Wiggles out of his cage very carefully, keeping one hand underneath, and put him safely in his run. Topsy cleaned out the hutch and put in fresh straw.

Topsy filled Wiggles' dish with oats
and bran and put clean water in his
drinking bowl. Mummy gave Tim
some apple, carrots and lettuce
leaves to put in Wiggles' run.

While Topsy and Tim were playing
with Wiggles, Josie Miller came to
see them. She was carrying her
hamster cage.
"Please will you look after Lily
for me?" she said. "I'm going away
on holiday for a week."

Topsy and Tim ran to ask
Mummy if they could.
"All right," said Mummy,
"but Josie must tell you how
to look after a hamster."

Josie gave them a packet of hamster
food. "You must fill Lily's dish every
evening," she said.
"She also likes bits of apple, carrot,
lettuce or cabbage, and she loves nuts!"

Just then, Lily popped out of her
nest box and went to her food dish.
"Isn't she eating a lot!" said Tim.
"She isn't eating it," said Josie.
"She's filling the pouches in her
cheeks. Then she will put the food
in her food store to eat later."

Josie asked Topsy and Tim to clean
out Lily's food store every other day,
so that it didn't get smelly.
"And please will you fill her water
bottle every day," said Josie.
"I'll do that!" said Topsy.

"She's got an exercise wheel like Tubby's," said Tim.

"Yes," said Josie. "You'll hear her playing in it at night-time."

Just then, Tubby climbed into his wheel and had a spin.

"Lily will have a lovely time with Topsy and Tim and their pets," said Mummy. "Goodbye, Lily," said Josie. "Have a good holiday with Topsy and Tim!"

Topsy+Tim

The New Baby

Topsy and Tim were having tea with
Tony Welch. Tony's mum was going
to have a baby. It was growing in
her tummy.

Tony put his hand on his mum's
big tummy.
"I can feel the baby moving," he said.
Tony's mum let Topsy and Tim feel her
tummy too.
"Ooh!" said Topsy. "It kicked my hand."

"When will the baby be born?"
asked Tim.
"In a week or so,"
said Tony's mum.
"I hope it's a girl,"
said Topsy.

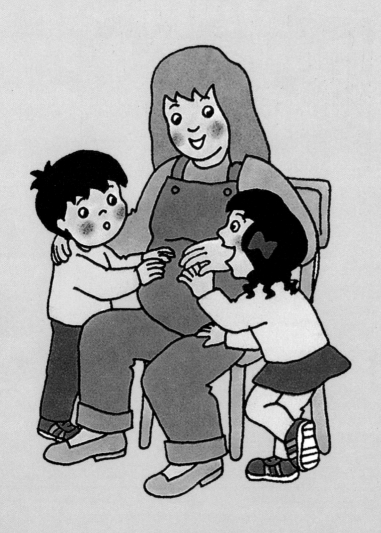

Later, Tony took Topsy
and Tim upstairs to see the
new baby's bedroom.
"I'm going to let it sleep in
my old cot," he said.

Topsy and Tim had brought a bag of
their old baby clothes for the new
baby. They helped Tony's mum
to put the clothes away in
a drawer.

One morning, Tony came to school looking very pleased.

"I've got a baby brother," he told the class. "He was born in the night and he's called Jack."

"You are lucky," said Topsy and Tim.

"Yes," said Tony. "I haven't seen him yet because he was born in hospital but Daddy is taking me there after school."

The next day, Tony came to
play with Topsy and Tim.
He was carrying a new car.
"Jack gave it to me,"
he told them.
"Can we see
Jack?" asked Tim.

"We'll go and meet Jack next week," said Mummy, "when Tony's mum brings him home." "What's he like?" asked Topsy. "He's very little and he cries a lot," said Tony.

Topsy and Tim talked about Jack all
week long. When Saturday came,
Mummy took them to see him.

"Can I hold him?" asked Topsy.
She sat on the floor and Tony's mum
put him on her lap. He felt very warm.
"I want to hold him, too," said Tim.

Jack began to cry. Tony's mum
picked him up.
"Why is he crying?" asked Tim.
"Babies don't know how to talk, so
they cry when they need something,"
said Tony's mum.

"He's pooed his pants," said Tony.
"No, he hasn't," said his mum.
"Perhaps he's hungry,"
said Topsy.
"I think you're right,"
said Tony's mum.

Tony's mum started to feed Jack.
He stopped crying and made loud
sucking noises.
"I want a drink, too," said Tony.

"There are some cartons of juice in
the fridge, Tony," said his mum.
"I expect Topsy and Tim would
like a drink too."

After they'd finished their
drinks, Topsy and Tim and
Tony went to play football
in the garden.

When they came back in, Tony's mum
was changing Jack's nappy. Topsy and
Tim stood and watched.

"Now I'm going to give Jack his bath,"
said Tony's mum. "Would you like to
help me, Tony?"
Tony shook his head.

Topsy and Tim played with Jack
while Tony's mum put warm water in
the baby bath and tested it with her
elbow to make sure it was not too hot
for Jack.

When she put Jack in the bath, he began to cry.
"He doesn't like the water," said Tim.
"Yes, he does," said Tony.

He lifted the baby's sponge and squeezed some water on to Jack's toes.

Jack stopped crying and gurgled.

"He's laughing," said Topsy.

"That's because he likes his big
brother," said Tony's mum and she
gave Tony a hug.

"Isn't Tony lucky to have a little
brother," said Topsy on the way home.
"I think Jack's lucky to have a big
brother like Tony," said Tim.